THIS BLOOMSBURY BOOK

BELONGS TO

....

Bloomsbury Publishing, London, Berlin and New York

First published in Great Britain in 2009 by Bloomsbury Publishing Plc
36 Soho Square, London, W1D 3QY

First published in Belgium and the Netherlands in 2009 by Clavis Uitgeverij,
Hasselt-Amsterdam

Text and illustrations copyright © 2009 Clavis Uitgeverij, Hasselt-Amsterdam
All rights reserved

Text and illustrations by Guido van Genechten
The moral right of the author/illustrator has been asserted

Original title:
Mag ik eens in je luier kijken?

A CIP catalogue record of this book is available from the British Library

ISBN 978 1 4088 0019 5

Printed in China

1 3 5 7 9 10 8 6 4 2

www.bloomsbury.com/childrens

GUIDO VAN GENECHTEN

Peek-a-Poo
What's in your nappy?

BLOOMSBURY

LONDON BERLIN NEW YORK

This is Mouse.
Mouse likes to investigate everything
and poke his nose everywhere . . .

He peeks into every hole he sees . . .

He looks inside jars
and under rocks . . .

Nothing is safe from inquisitive Mouse.

And there's something he needs to know.
Without blushing, Mouse asks his friend Rabbit,
'Rabbit, can I look in your nappy?'

'Go ahead,' says Rabbit, intrigued.

'I can see seven rabbit pellets,' says Mouse. 'One, two, three, four, five, six, seven!'

Next, Mouse scampers over to Goat and asks, 'Goat, can I look in your nappy?'

'Yes, you can,' Goat says, and she holds her arms up in the air to help Mouse.

'Just what I thought!' Mouse laughs.
'Goat droppings. Lots of them!'

With Doggy, Mouse is feeling bolder.
'Let me see in your nappy, please!'

'If you really want to,'
Doggy giggles.

'Aha!' Mouse says.
'One poo, with
a pointy end.'

Now Mouse is unstoppable.

'Hey, Cow, can I look inside your nappy, too?'

'Sure!' says Cow proudly.

'One big fresh cow pat,' Mouse nods. 'I should have known.'

'Hello, Horse,' Mouse says.
'Can I examine your nappy?'

'Oh, why not,' Horse mutters, just a tiny bit surprised.

'Three horse droppings,' Mouse grins. 'One, two, three.'

Piggy is last.
'Piggy,' asks Mouse, 'please
can I look inside your nappy?'

'Errrm . . . yes . . .'
Piggy blushes timidly.

'Wow!' says Mouse,
trying not to hold his
nose. 'I count one,
but it is quite smelly.'

By now, Rabbit, Goat, Doggy, Cow, Horse and Piggy are all terribly curious.

'Hey Mouse!' they ask.
'Can we look in YOUR nappy?'

'Of course!' Mouse says confidently.

'Oooh!' everyone cries out in surprise.

'Your nappy is empty!'

'How can that be possible?!'

'Easy!' Mouse explains.
'I don't use my nappy any more – I use a potty.'

'See! Here it is.'

'We want to try too!'
they all cry.